Miss Grégor is a translation of a French flagellant novel written by Alphonse Momas (1846-1933), a prolific author of erotica (*Miss Grégor*, London-Paris [Paris]: Société des Bibliophiles, 1907). Momas used numerous pseudonyms, including, amongst others, Tap-Tap, Pan-Pan, Trix, Fuckwell, and Le Nismois. *Miss Grégor* is part of Momas' series, 'Par le fouet et par la verge' — 'By whip and by rod.' It is also the second book in a three volume series set in an elite girls' school in London governed by a harsh disciplinarian, Miss Sticker. The other books in this series are *Miss Mary* (1907) and *Le Secret de Miss Sticker* (1907).

This Birchgrove Press edition of *Miss Grégor* is based on an English translation first published in 1907 (*Miss Grégor*, London-Paris: Privately printed for the French and English Bibliophiles Society). It was most probably published and printed in France and, given the idiosyncratic nature of the translation, was almost certainly translated by someone whose first language was not English.

Chapter headpiece decorations in this Birchgrove Press edition of *Miss Grégor* are from another flagellant novel written by Momas, *Fouetteuse*, par Trix (Paris-Bruxelles, 1901). Chapter tailpiece decorations are based on designs in *Fouetteuse*.

The English translation of *Miss Mary* (London-Paris, Privately printed for the French and English Bibliophiles Society, 1906 [c. 1907]) is also available from Birchgrove Press.

By whip and by rod

Miss Grégor

BY

TAP-TAP

LONDON-PARIS

Privately printed for the French and English

BIBLIOPHILES SOCIETY
1907

BIRCHGROVE PRESS
MMXII

Miss Grégor
© The British Library Board P.C.13.ff.25

© Birchgrove Press
2012

ISBN:
978-0-9871953-7-1

http://www.birchgrovepress.com

Miss Grégor

BY

TAP-TAP

BY WHIP AND BY ROD

MISS GRÉGOR

BY

TAP-TAP

CHAPTER I

Miss Gregor had the supervision of the 3ᵈ class where the pupils were ranging from thirteen and one half to 15 years of age. There were twelve in number and Reine de Glady was amongst them.

The School was a big square, on the ground floor, at the back of the building, right over the gardens.

The pupils had desks in which they kept their books, like in all other schools, but each desk was separated from the other allowing the teacher to circulate around it, and to come and sit near the pupil so as to question her about her lessons.

The classes were taught in the morning and afternoon, in two divisions.

Reine belonged to the morning division and spent her afternoon taking lessons in fancy work and riding: she took three riding lessons a week.

She was taking a riding lesson the day this story begins, and her place was empty in the school. This absence tormented Miss Gregor who was all the time looking at the window on the side where she expected her to come back.

Three months had passed since the vacation and Miss Gregor had greatly changed in looks and ways.

She was thinner through the fever that burned her, her eyes were getting black underneath, her face was white, and her shoulders were drooping: she could not keep quiet a quarter of an hour walking about among the girls, approaching one and then another, hardly looking at the work, but giving all her attention to Reine, always advising her often, embracing her around the waist, rubbing against her, and leaving her only with regret.

All the girls had noticed it and looked maliciously at one another, for these children did not stop at suppositions now, but understood well the motive guiding such impressions on their teacher.

Noticing Miss Gregor looking so much through the window, troubled and anxious, awaiting the return of Reine, the girls were all smiling and there was a general air of carelessness noticeable among the larger ones, an attitude that would have terrified the strict Miss Sticker herself.

Reine's neighbour on the right seemed to be more distracted than any other: she was a nice looking girl, with ginger-hair, about 15, tall and well formed, with an aquiline nose, and a charming face.

Miss Alexandra Corsiger — was her name — had nervous movements in the legs which could be seen under her short skirt. But now Miss Gregor was leaving the window to look at the pupils, and Alexandra pretended to work hard.

Impatiently, the teacher opened the door that communicated with a vestibule and left the school-room to itself.

As quick as lightning, Alexandra opened Reine's desk and threw a note in it, her neighbour smiling murmured:

— She'll read it.

The girl's heart was beating hard; she was very pale, while bringing her eyes down on her paper, as she saw Miss Gregor entering the room again.

The teacher had gone to the window, and was full of joy, and sighing with satisfaction.

A few seconds after, Reine entered smiling.

Miss Gregor had altered, we said, but what a transformation in the French girl so sad and timid at first!

Reine had the same light-grey dress as her companions wore, the same short skirt, not much below the knees, which was the class uniform. A red ribbon was tied round the neck and a gold medal, for good study hung from it! Her hair was arranged any how, her eyes were brilliant and always looking right into the eyes of the person talking to her, her smile was vivacious, she looked the image of a perfect little devil in the model school of Miss Sticker.

— You were long coming from the riding-school, observed Miss Gregor.

— The lesson was interesting, Miss, and I was asked to bring back to school little Miss Herbert.

— So? And I had something to communicate to her teacher. You should have brought her here with you.

— I couldn't guess! Why don't you go? You know you are liked in our school, and that we work even harder when you are not with us.

— Yes, and I'll go in a moment. Take your seat, and let me see first if your work does not suffer from all other arts you are learning.

Reine smiled. It was the same thing every time she came back from the riding-lesson. Miss Gregor always used to run and question her. She went to her desk, and Miss Gregor went indifferently to the window, as she had done before Reine's arrival, so as not to give any suspicions to the pupils, but she did not see the look and smile her

« gougnotte » was exchanging with some pupils, putting her tongue between her lips.

Reine sat down. Alexandra made a motion of the eyes to her desk and Reine, nodding, opened it, took the note and put it in a book, but had time to read:

« Oh Reine, I was told what you do is so good I want to taste it! I have prepared my self! As soon as Miss Gregor will be gone out, I'll tend you my legs. I am afraid, but I must know your caresses, and I think I'll love you with fury. »

She hid the letter in her pocket, turned her head towards Alexandra, and her eyes said: yes!

Miss Gregor, of course had seen nothing: she came near her favored pupil, sat by her, and for one moment contemplated her with eyes mad with lust: the girl had so much taken hold of her senses! She followed her writing, and said:

— All right, Reine, I am pleased. You work, losing no time: I shall only have praises for you.

— I'll always try to satisfy you, Miss.

Miss Gregor shivered with volupty under her meaning look and movement of the lip.

She was frightened to give herself away and continued:

— I'm going to Miss Tokal's division. I rely on you for the survey: the whip to those who shall have disturbed the order.

Behind Miss Gregor's desk, one could see the whip hanging under the wording: By whip and by rod! this threat was worse this year as teachers had been permitted to give immediately the flagellation to any unruly pupil.

— Be sure, Miss, answered Reine, none of these young ladies will have to have it. This is the model division.

— Too model, murmured the teacher, going to the door.

She was not gone a second, when Alexandra turned her seat towards Reine, who said to another girl.

— Lisbeth, look out!

Without another word, Reine went down before Alexandra and told her to pull up her dress. The girl trembled and had only raised it up, showing her thighs: Reine was no more timid, and with decision, she pulled it right up on the belly. One could now see white and plump thighs that Reine opened with her hands and saw a golden pussy, a fresh and genteel cunt.

— Non, your legs round my neck, ordered she.

But she was obliged to put them there herself, so the girl was timid, and then she put her gourmand mouth on the clitoris and sucked it with passion.

— Ah! ah! ah! exclaimed Alexandra, enough, it tickles me too much. I'm dying, you kill me! She put her legs quickly away leaving Reine silly and ready to be cross.

— Silly, is that all that you wanted? What's the good writing me love letters? Miss Gregor will be back and I shall have lost my time. May, turn over and take her place!

— I also, I also, murmured many voices.

— Shut up!

May who was on Reine's left, stood up, and her skirts up to the waist, brought her thighs in contact with Reine's face, as she was still kneeling. She gave her a few licks, after having opened her drawers and murmured:

— Give me your bottom: you prefer caresses there. I'll give you a few tongue licks and I'll pass to two others.

A tall dark-haired girl had left her seat and came forward, skirt right up, drawers all open, and two more girls, behind her, did the same.

Reine was giving clever « feuilles de rose » to May's nice bottom-hole, and also a few licks to the cunt, saying:

— Snough! go to your desk, for miss Gregor might come back.

Alexandra had lost all countenance remaining with her skirts on her knees, and a tear fell from her eyes, as she was sorry to have lost the sensation she was told about and she thought of experiencing ever so much more, because she was in love with Reine.

Reine sent the others away and turning to Alexandra, said:

— Don't cry, I'll try once more, and if you are ticklish, I'll denounce you to miss Gregor, for having been troublesome. You'll receive the whip and I'll prepare you for my caresses.

— No, no! don't denounce me! She would see I have no drawers, she would report it and God knows what would be the consequences.

Reine kneeled to place herself between Alexandra's thighs, put her legs over her neck again, and began by little kisses on the cunt: the heat that reigns in these forbidden regions excited the « gougnotte », who played with pussy and clitoris, sent in a timid tongue, getting more and more audacious, as the tender pressure of the thighs was felt on the cheeks of her face.

Alexandra's heart was full of voluptuous passion; the dark-haired girl who was behind Reine, said:

— So pull up your skirts, Alexandra, Reine's head is always underneath, the blood is sure to go to her head, and it would give the game away.

Shutting her eyes, Alexandra, under the excitement, pulled up her dress without any reserve, and May as well as the dark-haired girl could see the marvellous play of Reine's tongue on the most secret sexualities and the most profound folds.

How knowing that French girl's tongue was, indeed! Reine noticing the attention turned her head, making a most suggestive grimace of lust.

— What a pig, that French girl is, said May! and one always wants it with her.

— But Lisbeth gave the alarm: Miss Gregor!

It was a vertiginous execution: all girls resumed their seats, working hard in their books, when the teacher entered:

— Silence has been observed, said she, very well.

A shiver went round the room, when the girls noticed Reine putting the top of her penholder to her mouth — a sure sign of denunciation.

— Ah, said Miss Gregor, approaching Reine, a fault has been committed. Who was it?

— Miss May, announced Reine, has pronounced disdainfully the words: French Girl!

— Really? said May. Reine looked right in her eyes and asked:

— Did you say it or not? Am I a liar and shall I have to be punished? Well I am sorry.

— I did say it, Miss Gregor, answered May humbly. I am sorry for it. I beg pardon to Reine.

— One must never insult a companion's

country. Come here, Miss May, and I'll whip you.

— Oh, please, don't. I'm certain Reine will intercede.

— Come here, I tell you. Or shall I go to Miss Sticker?

— Oh, no!

— As you submit, your punishment will be slight and you won't have to show your bottom to your friends. Look at them and support your punishment with resignation. Pull up your skirts and get your cheeks out of your drawers. Be quick or I'll ask Reine and Alexandra to hold up your arms, I'll pin your skirts to the shoulders, and before all the division, I'll whip you till you bleed.

May did what she was told, and soon showed her two nice little apples, that she liked Reine so much to lick. Fearing that the whip should hit her finger she opened the sides of the drawers as much as she could.

Miss Gregor held up the whip, and it come down, beating the flesh in such way that the girl oscillated on her feet, but did not cry.

— Are you no more solid than that, Miss May? Let us see if other blows will give you more vigor.

Four times the whip came down, the cheeks shutting and opening at each blow. May wept, but did not cry out, as she was afraid her punishment would be known to Miss Sticker.

The last blow, the sixth one was not so hard, more of a caress, because she had supported all calmly. The cheeks however were red and painful, and May could not sit down for a while.

She addressed a reproachful look at Reine who impassible, was still at work.

Miss Gregor had resumed her seat at her desk, surveying the whole class in general, but noticing Reine only, in reality. The girl's influence over her heart and soul was greater than she ever thought it could be!

She felt now that she was no more governing her school and simply lost her mind desiring that French girl of whom she became horribly jealous. She was watching carefully, afraid that the would run after some big girl, Mary perhaps or some other teacher — although she knew she was the only one among the teachers to be at fault — and by a strange blinding of passion,

she never had an idea that her little
« gougnotte » could have sought her own
companions! For her, they were only
children without importance.

Had she been afraid of anything concern-
ing Reine with companions, it would have
been with those of lower classes that Reine
would perhaps be inclined to debauch,
guiding their perverse instincts. She knew
Reine was vice itself, that she was more and
more ardent in the manifestation of her
desire, that she loved woman and would
certainly love other petticoats.

The teacher objected sometimes to certain
liberties taken by Reine's companions but
the French girl was clever enough to attract
punishments to these girls, so as to take all
suspicions away: she went even as to ask the
teacher to move them away from her desk.

Reine knew what power she had over
Miss Gregor, enjoyed it and even abused it, a
cause of bad feelings on the part of her
companions.

When back from Scotland after the scene
with Anna, they stopped their love affairs
for a while, for Miss Sticker's sister had been
added to the staff, a younger but married

sister who pretended that although the severity was to be maintained, the girls should have more latitude in their acquaintance, so as to enter the world with more liberty in their ways, like American girls.

Recreations were organised, chatting allowed, and from that moment did Miss Gregor become jealous, noticing Reine chatting sometimes with Mary. She kept quiet, where she learned that such intimacy was to seek opportunities for Mary and Anna's punishments. She then admired her little « gougnotte » and kept her for herself under pretence of pushing her in her studies.

Reine only wanted to satisfy her in her lust, pursuing her incessantly by her solicitations, joining her by night and day, asking her for rendez-vous anywhere to suck her, and such solicitations were warning up Miss Gregor, who committed imprudences, such as to lock herself with Reine in the w. c. to make her suck her clitoris and vagina, and come quick. And she came, nearly ready to die, Reine was really pumping all the juice out of her veins.

Fatigues at the time of the periods

brought a break in their relations, and Reine, who liked to be endlessly begged to come to the teacher's desk to whisper loving words, noticed her companions had tried to pierce the mystery of her power over Miss Gregor. From then she knew that all wills would be submitted to her luxury, as soon as she would like it.

She conceived a plan, watching all those girls trying to know her great secret.

English girls, although cooler, so as to better play with hypocrisy, pudery and chastity, understand all the same the sin of luxury.

It first happened with that dark-haired girl we mentioned before, Miss Eva Normans.

Miss Gregor was then carefully reading a note sent to her by Miss Sticker, when Reine looking at Eva right in the eyes made a sign with her tongue passed between the lips: the girl blushed, moved the head, let her understand she knew and would not mind it.

As is often the case, opportunity offered itself at once to prove if they really understand one another.

A servant called for Miss Gregor to go to Miss Sticker at once. Without any apprehension Miss Gregor went, and Eva whispered to Reine.

— What do you want with your tongue?

— Pull up your skirt, open your drawers, you'll see. All the neighbouring companions were stupefied, as they saw Eva obey.

— No denunciation, you know, said Reine imperatively.

There was no fear they should think of such thing.

They were all curious, trying to see between Eva's opened legs. The chemise was right up and showed the young pussy. Reine kneeled, enveloped by the skirts, approached her head near Eva's pussy, seemed to kiss it with pleasure, and then before all girls astonished, and bending down to follow the show, she applied her mouth on Eva's cunt, licked it, brought the tongue right up on the clitoris and sucked it.

An indescribable feeling took possession of all the girls' hearts. Reine experienced a wonderful pleasure in looking at Eva, multiplying the work of the tongue and the sucks, by the feeling of the hands and that

Eva was having her share of enjoyment also, the smile on her lips showed. More, more than ever was she pushing her parts towards Reine's caresses, pressing her head with her hands, to keep it between her thighs. Suddenly a contraction was evident, she was coming, and murmured: « Oh, how nice! »

The French girl was still kneeling and Eva went back to wipe herself with her hand-kerchief; another girl approached now, in the same posture, with her skirts up, saying:

— Do it to me too, Reine.

Reine turned back, still kneeling, and started licking that other cunt, it did not come but showed its pleasure by a comical movement of the belly.

After that all resumed work, so as not to be caught by miss Gregor.

From that moment Reine managed to have all the girls moved one after another to the two desks at her sides. The last one of all was Alexandra.

Reine was licking with passion — all these young cunts which were offered to her lips, these cheeks moving under her caresses, these looks courting her, every-thing was charming her mind and senses, but she was more enamoured of miss Gregor, who was a woman. Miss Gregor was now calling Reine, asking for her work to examine, and the girl obeyed at once.

The teacher resting her own head on one elbow, fixed Reine right in the eyes, took the book, and asked:

— What is written there? You did not think much about your work, it seems!

Reine bent down and her ear being level with miss Gregor's lips, this one whispered:

— Kneel down and beg my pardon!

CHAPTER II

At this culminating point an erotical mentality, decided to brave anything to satisfy the desire wringing the senses; for the sceptics, ready to call impossible what is to follow here, it is well to examine the minds of the creatures occupying the school-room and to detach this soul *alone*, uniting all intelligences in a momentaneous current of mutual aspirations.

Indeed there was no community of thought between miss Gregor and her pupils. She still thought herself the only lustful being using Reine's perversity, and that the girls had no idea of their lesbian relations. But the breath of impurity that was brought by Reine in miss Sticker's school, developed right and left, catching each one. Already, nearly one third was contaminated, but that third curiously did not turn to contaminate the other two-thirds, but was contented, being under the power of the French girl.

Amongst the girls, there were the « called » and the « elected » and the last named formed around Reine a sort of guard of honor, preventing her to escape to other divisions. They kept her like a precious treasure. Miss Gregor liked it but was far from knowing the true motive of such union.

Now, miss Gregor was encircled by a sort of mist, coming out of all the sexual heat of the desire emanating from the girls, and instinctively felt herself giving way to her feelings of lust.

Before her that mouth, smiling, defying, true poem of piggish acts, was exciting her terribly. She wanted it glued to her vagina, to absorb all the wet that was going to be precipitated by it. She struggled no more against herself; she glanced at the school, and seeing all heads bent down on the books, she called her « gougnotte ».

— Kneel down and beg my pardon, she

had said to Reine.

She had read in the teacher's eyes the impossibility of delaying any longer the coming. She obeyed, and kneeling down:

— Pardon me, miss Gregor, I had a distraction.

Three pupils held their head up, and miss Gregor said:

— If any one of you show the least curiosity, I send her to miss Sticker under prevention of rebellion: you'll know what it will cost you.

No threat was necessary. The contracted hearts were languid now, knowing the act wanted by the teacher. They did not want to see with the eyes, the hearts could guess and were therefore in communion with the teacher. They were all living the scene that was being enacted.

Let those who read this, scrutinise the far away past of their youths. Débauché teachers, precocious pupils in lust have always existed, and always and everywhere the venerian act has been committed, against all severities and interdictions.

Miss Gregor had pushed her armchair back, and the table-cover, covering the whole of the legs of the table, hid all her movements. At once she pulled up skirts and chemise right up to her breast, and, as there were no drawers in the way, the legs wide open let the cheeks come right to the edge of the seat and the belly appeared as white as a lily, with the navel and the pussy thick and well furnished.

She forced Reine on her cout. The girl approached her lips and put her hands under the bottom. The sensation was maddening for the teacher who closed her eyes and bit her own finger so as not to utter a cry of lust.

Reine's mouth was over the whole of the cout, sending in only a discreet tongue: the thighs were now pressing the face, and she began to lick all round the sexual lips, going deep into the pussy, finding the clitoris and sucking it. The pleasure came, at once, irresistible, so much so that miss Gregor, throwing her legs right over Reine's shoulders, glued the face on her vagina wet with love's dew.

Was she dead? Her eyes were closed, the head was falling back and the hair all undone. She was coming, coming, she had come now, her legs and feet were falling on the floor, brought down gently by Reine's hands, to prevent a too violent shock. She was motionless, and the French girl, the head on her thighs, was tossing her off with an expert finger, kissing the cout all the time, and licking the spunk that filtered out. The pleasure was beginning again.

The teacher was killing herself, and her « gougnotte » like a vampire attached to her flesh, did not get fatigued of kissing, licking, sucking...

At last her hand pressed the girl's head so as to stop, and Reine obeyed. Now miss Gregor was getting up slowly and coming to her senses. She glanced over the school, every one was working studiously.

— Reine, said she, I forgive you. Go back to your seat. I want some fresh air and will go for a minute to the garde gate. Don't let me hear any sound of conversation.

Reine did what she was ordered: her hair was a bit disheveled. Miss Gregor arranged her own, and before leaving the room, approached Reine, looked her in the eyes, smiled, and said:

— To reward my leniency, darling, I rely

on you to keep the school in good order during my absence.

— Sure, miss Gregor.

The teacher wanted not only air, but also to freshen her bottom and to calm her excitement, the French girl understood her absence should be longer than she thought: her perversity at once turned to some other subject. If she liked to be a « gougnotte », she came seldom herself, and only at night, after being full up with miss Gregor. She was profiting more than she was losing.

Miss Gregor gone out, Reine took a small mirror out of her desk, smiled to herself, and arranged her hair. A gentle cough, near by, made her turn her eyes towards Alexandra. She did not hesitate, but put down the mirror, knelt down, and said:

— Pull up your dress, I'll start again with you.

This time Alexandra knew better and obeyed at once, bringing her thighs herself to the « gougnotte's » lips.

The tongue worked a while with rapidity, then stopped, and Reine ordered Alexandra to stand up.

This she did. Reine began again, and with

her finger felt for the bottom-hole, into which she pushed it. The empaled one uttered a cry that was stopped with the pleasure coming. The beautiful fair one must have wanted it badly, for Reine could not dry her with the tongue: it was running, always running.

— I'm tired out, murmured Alexandra, sitting down at her desk, while Reine still kneeling was wiping her lips to take all trace of moisture away.

No one took any notice now: it was natural.

— Were you satisfied? Have you come nicely?

— Oh, yes! I did not expect such a sensation!

The dark-haired girl observed now:

— You have the devil in you to make us come so!

— Or to make one be whipped, intervened May.

— Ungrateful girl, said Reine, have you not the pluck to repay me the pleasure I give you, by a few blows, when I am displeased, it will be all over between us.

— Oh, Reine! I'm not cross but my cheeks

are all scratched by the whip and I should prefer your tongue on them.

— I had to invent something, so that miss Gregor should not suspect anything.

— You're an Angel, murmured Alexandra, who got up and embracing her, kissed her on the lips.

— You'll understand what love means.

— Keep quiet at your desks, said the dark-haired girl, for miss Gregor cannot be far.

— At least another five minutes, interrupted Reine.

— Are your sure? Oh, say, do it to me again.

— Right. I am always ready, but I am afraid it will fatigue you and would be noticed.

— Caress me on the other side.

— You want to know the effect of my tongue on your bottom?

— Yes, said Alexandra, pulling her dress up and turning her cheeks, showing a nice little bottom, full and plump with an exciting slit well open.

Reine was at work at once, kissing the cheeks first, then biting them with the mouth and going then through the slit, up and down, licking and putting a finger right in the hole. Alexandra jumped:

— Quicker, yes, it is so good! oh darling Reine!

— Shut up, cried the dark-haired girl, be quick! or we'll all get excited, and won't be reasonable! miss Gregor will then take us all at fault.

— Yes, enough, joined in Reine getting up. You know the two ways now; when you like, we'll do it again.

— Presently we shall have to take numbers, said May.

— No need, my tongue works well and can satisfy you all.

Fortunately the two girls had resumed their seats, for miss Gregor was entering again, calmer, although her eyes were darker and more amorous in her face so pale. She came straight to Reine:

— Have you all been good?

Alexandra had a great trouble, noticing the undecided look in Reine's eyes: but it was only a wrong idea.

— We worked, miss, and had no time for distraction. Besides we did not wish to displease you.

The teacher took her hand and pressed it tenderly. She sighed and went back to her desk.

She would have never thought that this child should have infused such passion in her. It was all through the mutual danger they had run on account of Anna, that they were now so much bound to one another. But they still meant to have their revenge, and Reine counted on her lovers, whom she trained to know Anna's doings.

The little French girl, sent away from France for immorality and put in miss Sticker's strict school, exerted now her influence on all those who approached her, and could fight against the hostility of Anna, held in esteem by all for her great wealth.

Lustful thoughts were continually in Reine's heart and if she worked with assiduity to content the teachers, she was proud of the power she had over the girls whose senses she had awakened. She knew she was looked to for the pleasure of her caresses, she was pleased with the love letters she received, of the smiles she attracted and which curiously miss Gregor did not catch.

Alexandra had been satisfied, she had come, and knew of the piggish art of the French girl. She kept looking and smiling at her and, having dropped a pencil, she gave another note to Reine.

« I am happy, happy, said she in it, Reine of my heart, for we'll soon begin again, and I won't be ticklish any more. »

Reine nodded: for ever and for ever would she put her head under her companions' skirts.

At recreation time it was raining, one could not go in the garden and the pupils had to stay then in an immense hall or in a gallery adorned with glass windows. If it was dark the pupils stopped in the schoolroom but had access to the vestibule; the teacher put down on a list the refreshments they wanted for 4 o'clock and left them to give the list at the office, and a servant brought them afterwards on a tray.

That day, besides the rain, the clouds were very dark and miss Gregor had just gone with the list.

There would have been an opportunity for a new edition of « minettes » for

Alexandra, but she had joined another girl who had received a letter from her parents. And Reine was trying some new crochet stitch. The pupils were by groups, and Reine alone did not join any group. Lisbeth whispered to the dark-haired girl.

— Hullo! Reine, does not take advantage of the opportunity.

It was like gun-powder. All turned round:

— She has been changed, said May, for once she is not after us.

— Hullo! Reine, said another, don't you appreciate any longer the little piggish ways?

Reine looked up and smiled:

— It's no use starting.

— Because you would have no time to get under all dresses.

— What for?

— A little lick, so as to know all our differences and you would only have to choose what you fancied. There would always be one of us disposed for it.

Reine thought a moment, saw all the eyes full of lust at such proposition.

— Yes, I'll have time for one lick at all your bottoms. Get in row pull up your skirts, you'll see if I forget any one!

Two pupils stopped in the vestibule, on the watch, but looking also on what was happening in the school-room. Rapidly all dresses were up, all drawers were open, and bottoms presented themselves of varied shapes, round, plump, pointed, curved, massive, etc.: and one could hear lots of ah! oh! light blows on the flesh, Reine on all fours stopped at each pair of legs, gave a sound kiss on the white spheres, licked in all the length of the slit, and sometimes put a finger on the clitoris, going after to the next one. The eleven pupils had it in succession: she got up at the last and said:

That's only a game, but if you are good comrades, I promise you you'll all come during the year.

She said it and meant it, and they all contemplated her with admiration. The dark-haired one even took her by the neck and kissed her.

At night she could not join miss Gregor as quickly as she wanted, for there was a meeting of all teachers under the presidency of miss Sticker, to examine the reports of all the pupils. And such meetings lasted always up to 10 o'clock.

Reine went to her own room, and undressing admired herself standing in front of her bed, remembering all the little cunts and bottoms which were now her pleasure machinery.

She was naked now, admiring her white belly, her growing pussy, her curved back, her breast beginning to stand up and point out; she felt for her clitoris, not to toss herself off, but to have conscience of all her beauties, because she liked more to work than to being worked.

And, in thought she came back always to the burning of miss Gregor, to her vulva swelling each time she touched it with her mouth, to her clitoris getting sometimes as big as the top of the little finger shivering while she bit it with her lips; to her bottom so strong with its thick slit where she dipped her nose and mouth in full.

It was long to wait. Not yet nine o'clock. Suddenly she heard a door opened with precaution.

What, Miss already? She turned her head, and was surprised: Alexandra was coming in, dressed in a petticoat and shawl only.

Reine was astonished! Fancy coming so at night, without saying a word, not knowing if it would please her or not! Alexandra entered, closed the door, knelt down, kissed Reine's knees, embraced her and murmured:

— I guessed you were the handsomest of us all. I wanted to see you and I've risked every thing to satisfy meself.

She was the first one to think about Reine's own beauty, that she had a body that could accept caresses, the first one, except miss Gregor — but with her she came for love, more than for piggish acts!

Although she had a preference for *working*, she was moved, and ever so much more, because the English girl was caressing her, turning her all over, so as to know her every where and mix not a few kisses with her caresses.

— You forgive me for having disturbed you?

— Yes, but you ought to have told me. You can't stay long.

— I guess you are miss Gregor's best friend, that you come together and go to bed together.

— What has it to do with you?

— All the others guess it, but nobody is jealous of you for it. We all like you passing under our skirts and licking, the rest is nothing to us. Say, is it so one licks?

Alexandra was pointing her tongue on Reine's cout, pressing the cheeks of her bottom with both her hands.

— Yes, but suck a little higher, you know, the little bud; I know, where's yours, come, I'll suck it and will teach you how to do it.

— A lick at your bottom to give you back what you did to mine.

— There it is, kiss it and lick it.

Reine put her bottom right on Alexandra's face: she played with it with her tongue, and all of a sudden, pushed her finger in the hole.

— Oh, you remember the lesson, said Reine, smiling.

Take everything off, even the chemise and come on my bed.

— All naked, I dare not, I have not your courage.

— Don't be silly, as you have come as far as here; to come nicely, there's nothing like being both naked: one sees one everywhere, nothing is in the way, one licks where one likes.

She helped her to undress, and when naked, examined her:

— You are very, very nice, Alexandra, you are almost the best formed of the school. Come quick on my bed, I'll make you come and you'll run away.

— You are expecting miss Gregor?

— Curious girl?

— Oh, there is an important meeting, I heard miss Clary say so: Gregor won't be here before half past ten.

— Ush! take me in your arms as I am taking you in mine.

Alexandra, obeying the instructions, they both embraced arms and legs, rubbing belly against belly. Alexandra soon shivered in the whole of her body, but the movements were growing and they played like two she-cats, trying to put clitoris over cunt. Reine, being more expert, more agile, put one thigh between those of her companion and rubbed her so much on her sexuality, that she came all over, half-dead: Now Reine had put her face on it, mouth over cunt and clitoris, kissing, licking, sucking, sending her into convulsions. As in the afternoon, Alexandra had a vivid pleasure, and wetted Reine's lips, while this one was swallowing the dew without stopping. When it was all over, the English girl remained annihilated before the French girl just as ardent as ever.

— There's no fatigue in you?

— You don't imagine how I love it. I seem to have in my body all the connings, so much I make others come. And I don't run. I come seldom, but my pleasure is lasting. Dress up now and go away.

— Yes, I'll go. Say, is it true you do it with Gregor?

— You are silly to ask it.

— You think one does not know you did it during School?

— And if I had you all whipped to-morrow?

— No, no, no such joke! Don't be spiteful, Reine, you were wrong about May.

— Get away, you are ready, and if we do not stop talking, I shall have to do it to you again, and to-morrow you would be ill.

— I have licked you, Reine!

— True! There, kiss my mouth, we shall have exchanged the kiss of love that I have not taught to others.

Such kiss turned to a tongue-touch and they separated. Reine put on her night-gown and waited for Miss Gregor to come and fetch her.

CHAPTER III

She was asleep, when the teacher came and kissed her.

— Don't wake up, darling, you want to sleep, and I'll go to sleep too. We'll talk to-morrow.

— No, no. I don't want to sleep, I was waiting for you impatiently, my little Gregor. I must suck you and enjoy your coming. Bring me to your room.

— Right. I want it as much as yourself; come up, and follow me without a noise.

The girl did what she was told, and they soon were in the teacher's room. Miss Gregor contemplated her with an amorous ecstasy, just as Alexandra had done a while ago.

— You are lovely, darling, with your hair done alas! you'll have to alter the dressing of your hair, Miss Sticker intends to forbid it, for other girls have been jealous of it. Let me see you the last time, with the air of a little devil it gives you.

— What! I shan't be able to keep my curls?

— The hair flat on the head, in the future, such is Miss Sticker's order: all contravention to it will be punished by the rod. Her sister Gertrie dissented but she would listen to nothing. Miss Sticker was very strong against you, and I have been in great fear, I tell you.

— Anna is at the bottom of it all! Oh! that we can find nothing for revenge.

Miss Gregor could not wait any longer, she simply undid her dress, laid on the bed, and the thighs right up, called her « gougnotte » :

— Begin quick, a few licks, we'll enjoy ourselves more afterwards.

Reine jumped on the open legs, with a rage even greater than if she had been deprived of it all the afternoon. But the more her tongue tasted the more desire she felt.

On her two knees, taking care to hold up Miss Gregor's bottom against her naked breast, while licking cunt and clitoris, she caressed also the cheeks, rubbing them on her own flesh, lost almost in the teacher's legs. The last one put her bottom on the calves of her own legs, to content her, got her back up, and Reine felt with volupty the vagina getting wet: her kisses went up then on the navel, stomach, and breast, while Miss was on her feet and hands, belly and bottom right up in the air, to give herself better to the girl's game.

It was not only lips, mouth and tongue which worked: with her arms she rounded the cheeks with her hands pressing the hips, and by the moving way of her legs, one could have sworn she tried to bugger her. The vagina was gaping, the clitoris getting up the vulva swelling, everything indicated the approach of the mad ecstasy: Miss Gregor was losing all senses under the voluptuous pleasure given her by Reine. Now she came, wetting, jumping on her bottom, biting the pillow so that her cries of excitement should not be heard out of the room.

— Reine, my treasure dear, my gem, love only me, think only of me, and when you'll be grown up I'll live on the very air you breathe in, I'll obey all your wills, you'll lick, suck me, night and day until I die, and I'll lick and suck you too! Reine my life, my mistress!

Such words fell like fire on the girl's soul. She continued, swallowing all the wet, and stopped only when both thighs pressed her head so, that she thought she would be crushed. A torpor succeeded to the excitement and Reine stopped the nose right in the vagina, while Miss Gregor seemed to await for another attack.

Little by little they managed to move, and miss Gregor finished undressing without leaving the bed. All naked now as well as Reine, she took her in her arms to kiss her on the mouth and asked her:

— Shall you always love my liquor?

— I shall never have enough of it.

— Have you any on your lips?

— I swallowed it all: put your tongue in my mouth perhaps will you find some in a corner.

They united their tongues, and the

teacher asked:

— Shall I make you come now?

— I prefer to always lick you! I want to suck the back now, after the front.

— You like it still?

— Oh yes, it is so nice.

— Get in quick.

Miss Gregor, laid on the back and her bottom, with its slit so well marked, fascinated Reine's looks. Soon she was at work on the « feuilles de rose » playing on it all the while with her fingers. She liked to make her shiver at the very simulacra of buggering, to see the cheeks moving about under the biting of her teeth on the lips of the hole, or to provoke the pleasure by putting the head on it and moving it between the thighs!

Little leech of volupty, she studied the places where kisses and caresses were acting more, bringing the shiverings to excess. From the bottom, she returned to the cunt, and from there to the nipples, she sucked also. Neither of them cried for mercy. The woman, dominated by the girl, gave her body away to lust, without any bound: the girl intoxicated with that body found in it the notion of sensual pleasures which would form her in the taste for lust.

When, exhausted, Miss Gregor felt round her neck the thighs of the girl, she did not even have the strength of putting her lips on it, but inhaled as one smells a bouquet of flowers, and murmured:

— Reine, I love you!

Her passion bent her before that child: she loved her to the death, and the delights of the flesh began again nearly every night up to midnight even later.

That night, however, Miss Gregor had some fear of something that may happen, and sent her away soon after midnight.

Reine covered with her cloak, was going quietly to her room. But nearing her room she saw a light in it, through the door. She fancied she had forgotten to close it firmly in her precipitation to follow Miss Gregor.

She went in, and was terrified to see Miss Sticker reading a note at the light of a lamp.

From that moment everything was like in a nightmare.

— Close your door, mademoiselle, said the school-mistress harshly, and tell me where you come from.

— From the w. c., Miss Sticker, I felt queer.

— Indeed, and you stayed there an hour or more? Will you kindly explain who sent you this very explicit letter, that I found in one of your dress pockets?

Reine remembered. It was Alexandra's note that she had forgotten to destroy.

— What letter, Miss? she asked innocently.

— You don't know that writing?

In her temper, Miss Sticker passed it under her eyes, but then, under a sudden impulse, without any fear of the correction to which she exposed herself, Reine took the letter abruptly and kept it in her hand, so that she could not take it back again.

— Give me that letter, said Miss Sticker!

— Never, Miss!

The school-mistress jumped on the girl, whose cloak rolled down on the ground, and who fought like a demon, so as to annihilate the document. Miss Sticker was pushing her to her bed so as to throw her on it. Reine noticing the move, struggled ever so much more and was then perfectly naked. She crumpled the letter still in her fingers, fell on her knees, while Miss Sticker fell behind her, holding her still between her legs, but in a rapid effort Reine managed to put her hand to her mouth and to swallow the letter.

— So, she said, you won't have it. Do with me as you please.

Miss Sticker, thunderstruck by such devotion to save an accomplice, dominated the fury, was tempted, incited, to give her a beating at once for such a fault against discipline.

The letter now swallowed, Reine stayed there on her fours, the head on her arms, bent on the bed, while her hips and legs were stuck between Miss Sticker's legs. An intense heat was all over her nakedness... but the school-mistress did not beat her. What was she doing then? Why did she not let her go? Why pass a hand to touch her nipples? What was she doing with her thighs breaching on them? Was she also giving way to the temptation of the flesh? A mad hope illuminated her mind, and she murmured:

— Pardon me, Miss Sticker. I am ready to repent.

Miss Sticker did not answer: her movements were more acute, while her breast was on Reine's back. Was it another unknown mode of flagellation? One hand was still on her nipples, her breath was tickling her shoulders, her lips were spitting on her neck.

— Mercy, mercy, pray, don't be cruel, I'll do what you like to merit your leniency. Shall I do it to you? Shall I make you come? I know you want it.

— Shut up, dirty girl, you would quicken my temper!

But her belly was still beating against Reine's cheeks, and the girl, on intuition, answered to such beating of the belly, and moved her cheeks about, flattening them against the body of the school mistress.

— Turn your head, said the latter, and let me see your young devil's face, and your hair every one talks about.

Instantly, Reine turned her head towards Miss Sticker: she thought herself sure of victory, she smiled, and made a motion with the tongue:

— Let me do it, I'm sure you'll pardon me.

The school-mistress' eyes showed the most burning lust, and the most superhuman efforts to dominate herself, and be contented with her belly beating on the cheeks.

One thing intrigued Reine in this strange duet: she felt something like a big corset point, round and thick going always towards the slit of her bottom, where it tried to get fixed. If it came up, Miss' hand always intervened to put it in place in the middle of her bottom, and the same if it went right or left.

Suddenly the school-mistress' thighs beat her bottom with violent trepidations: it seemed to her that the stays agitated convulsively: not knowing what it meant, Reine precipitated the beating of the bottom, rubbing herself like a cat under Miss, who pressed her between her arms which were around her breast, and who wetted her neck, and shoulders under a long caress.

— Miss, you see you want it. Let me do it, I'll make you so happy.

One of Miss Sticker's hands left her breast and went right underneath, tickling her bud.

— It is there, said Reine, guiding her finger on the clitoris.

But Miss Sticker hardly touched it, left the

hand flat against her thighs, observed a moment's quietness, got up and said:

— My mind is settled on your account, Miss Reine, you are a débauché, and to-morrow you'll receive the punishment you deserve.

The girl noticed the confused air of the school-mistress and could not help saying:

— You are committing an injustice: you jumped on me, and I can't give back to you the punishment to which you condemn me.

Miss Sticker smiled at the audacity of this girl who, proudly erect in her nudity had no shame; a sweet light was in her eyes, and Reine added:

— You struggle, Miss, you are wrong; I assure you it's very nice, and when once you have it done, you'll love me and will want me always.

— You're a pest in my house and I have engaged to keep you till the end of your schooling.

— You did not say so, just now, when your belly was caressing my bottom.

— Shut up, you unfortunate kid!

— It would have been much nicer, had you taken your dress and stays off.

A smile came to Miss Sticker's lips, and seeing the honour ribbon laying on Reine's dressing table, she passed it round her neck saying:

— If it was given for impudicity, you would wear it all your life time.

Reine had a moment of satisfaction, when she saw that ornament on her nakedness.

— You must confess it suits me.

Strange looks were in Miss Sticker's eyes; she still stopped looking at that damned French girl who stood before her, playing with hair, smile, lips and tongue. Reine had been too far, she counted upon victory, and was ready to pull up Miss Sticker's skirts when the latter recovering her reason, sent her back, saying:

— You express beautifully the comedy you are playing with me. I pretended to encourage you. Put your dressing gown on. I'll try to know your accomplice and such a scandal shall not occur again.

She opened the door and went out, leaving Reine astonished and terrified.

— Well, did she think after a while, there's an affair!

She has come, I'm certain of it. She

wanted it again, and then not. Go to the devil, Miss Sticker, I have swallowed the letter, shall tell in the morning Alexandra, and no one will know.

And getting in to bed, after putting her night-gown on, she went sleep.

CHAPTER IV

Anxiety was reigning in the school-room of Miss Gregor: Reine had had time to tell all her companions to deny everything. But all felt guilty and were in great trouble, as was also Miss Gregor who had received a note from Miss Sticker and dare not look at Reine or question her.

One felt a big event coming soon.

Half an hour before breakfast, Miss Sticker made her appearance, and approached the teacher at once.

— Miss Gregor, we have surprised one of the pupils of your division in a great fault. I have had a meeting of all the teachers and my sister. The culprit persists in not giving the name of her accomplice or accomplices.

The culprit is Miss de Glady. Her first punishment will be the whip before all her companions. To-night or to-morrow she'll be fustigated on the easel before all the pupils. We'll see after, if she still persists. You've heard, Miss Reine, will you speak.

— I've nothing to say.

— All right, come here, before your companions.

Reine left her place, joined Miss Sticker and stopped before her.

— Take your drawers off.

Without a word, she obeyed, and dropped the garment down, getting her feet out of it.

— Give me the whip, Miss Gregor, and pin her skirts to her shoulders.

Miss Gregor was ready to cry. She did however what she was told, while Reine was still smiling in a mocking manner. Her legs were naked, showing only her black stockings, and higher up one saw the well-shaped bottom. With one move Miss Sticker turned the cheeks of the girl's bottom towards her companions and said:

— Hold her by the shoulders, so that she won't try to escape.

— Sure I won't, answered Reine, as I am guilty I shall know how to bear my punishment.

At that moment Miss Sticker noticed she had still her honour-ribbon round the neck.

— What's this, Miss Gregor? You knew the child was guilty and you have not taken her ribbon away?

— I did not think for a moment my best pupil...

— Take it off at once!

Reine took it off herself and gave it to Miss Gregor.

Such delay left Reine in her posture a while longer before the pupils who contemplated her shape and blushed more or less, Alexandra and May especially, one because she had caressed them, the other because she noticed Reine's were nicer than her own.

— Mademoiselle, began Miss Sticker, I asked your teacher to make you stop that way of doing your hair. I confess I was wrong and I must agree with my sister Gertrie: your hair shows your character and will permit us to guess your thoughts which are unclean. Do you repent?

Miss Gregor, surprised at the length of time Miss Sticker waited to apply the whip, did not know what to do. She observed:

— Is the posture of the culprit not able to influence...

— What? said the school-mistress indignantly. If I make such an attitude last it is because I want to know if she will repent, and if her accomplice will denounce herself, diminishing in that way Reine's punishment, which would then be divided between the two.

— There's no accomplice, Miss Sticker, and if there was one, you would know her as well as I.

At such words, the whip went up and fell down on the poor little cheeks shivering from high and low.

— God! said Reine simply.

Miss Gregor held the shoulders in front, and she was as pale as death, feeling the blows more than the girl. The whip did not stop to beat and the flesh was glowing: Reine bit her lips not to cry and looked in Miss Gregor's eyes, and that gave her courage.

She understood how she loved her from

all her soul at the moment her unfaithfulness attracted on her the punishment of flagellation! Why did she not look at her severely? How nice she was to have still preserved her all her tenderness.

Reine could not know that she did not understand exactly the height of her fault and that at the bottom of her heart, she thought herself guaranteed by the silence of the culprit. Miss Gregor did not know Reine was also screening the other girls.

Miss Sticker's note given by the servant mentioned only that a young girl had been reported absent from her room for more than hour by the school-mistress herself, and that she must have been guilty of some great fault for which she would be punished in the morning.

Therefore, hearing Reine's name, she could not help admiring the girl who would so keep the secret of their passion.

Under the repeated blows of the whip, Reine trembled on her legs; the cheeks of her bottom marked with red marks began to bleed, she bent down, as ready to fall on Miss Gregor's lap; her back was getting round, higher up on the spine, and her pinned-up dress was making a slight noise: she moved her feet, and the calves of the legs were getting tight under the stockings, while the heel of the boot was kicking the floor, the hips were swinging, trying to evade the whip and the bottom ever so charming, seducing, was pinching itself so that the slit could hardly be seen.

Her courage was great, and if the eyes were crying silently, she was still smiling, and such smile went right to the heart of Miss Gregor.

The emotion was noticeable also on all the face of her companions; they were growing impatient, sorry or irritated. Alexandra was weeping, her hands over her eyes; Miss Eva Normans could hardly stop her irritation, and at last Lisbeth shouted:

— Pity, Madam, don't kill her.

Miss Sticker stopped beating and Reine fell in Miss Gregor's arms, taken by a crisis of tears: blood was coming down towards her stockings.

— It is atrocious, exclaimed Eva.

Then could Miss Sticker's voice be heard:

— Hullo! the culprits are denouncing themselves! Who weeps here? Miss de

Glady's desk neighbour? Ah! that's you Miss Alexandra Corsiger! And you also Miss Eva, Miss Lisbeth, Miss May! Why not all the school! Compliments to you, Miss Gregor!

The teacher could not speak. Lisbeth dared to reply:

— We are guilty of what, Miss Sticker? We don't know Miss Reine's fault! We can surely pity her, she is such a good comrade!

— The fault is in your conscience.

— We don't understand. If we are guilty of anything, we only ask to correct ourselves, but we must know first why we are culprits.

Before the courage of her pupils, Miss Gregor also spoke.

— I am sure of my pupils: if Miss Reine left her room, last night, as your note mentions, she might have forgotten herself, as all her country fellow-girls are sometimes flighty, and walk alone in the garden.

— In the rain? Are you losing your senses, Miss? Besides, I know better than any body else. I condescend to believe that the revolted-ones are not her accomplices, but I won't allow them to take the part of a culprit against my authority. Misses Eva and

Lisbeth, come over here and be whipped!

The two girls did not hesitate and came over at once.

— I'll be whipped gladly, if Miss Reine's punishment will then be put an end to.

— Are you giving orders here?

— No, but pray, Miss Sticker, hit me as hard as you like, but spare our companion.

— Her punishment is finished for this morning! Pull up your skirts, open your drawers, you'll receive four blows each for this time. Mind your fingers, or they'll be knocked too.

Lisbeth's garments up, she opened her drawers widely, and she showed a pair of round cheeks very genteel right above tiny legs. She was 14 years old and had golden hair. She was not troubled in her posture right in front of the whole of the school. The bottom came fully out of the drawers and it was noticeable Miss Sticker's four blows were not as hard as on Reine's bottom. It became red however.

It was Eva's turn, but she turned up her dress with less impatience.

— Shall I hit your hands? asked Miss Sticker.

Eva gave all liberty to her cheeks. They were higher on the legs, powerful, a very nice bottom indeed with thick cheeks and a deep slit. Miss Sticker considered it with more attention, looked at Reine, and seemed to think there might have been attraction. Eva did not move and received her beating.

Kneeling behind Reine, Miss Gregor wiped the blood, healed her cheeks and put some ointment on. The girl abandoned herself and did not weep any more. Miss Sticker spoke then:

— Let Miss de Glady's skirts fall down and give her back her drawers. This correction is nothing you know and it won't be noticed to-night. I give her till to-morrow, before using other corrective ways. I hope that by then, Miss Reine will have thought the matter over and decided to denounce her accomplice. For now, lock her up in the punishment room, and let her work and take her meals by herself. From time to time go and judge of her dispositions towards repentance. As regards you, young ladies, if the accomplice is amongst you and does not denounce herself, she'll receive a double correction.

The girls were terrified. Miss Gregor began to be surprised of such a threat on the part of the school-mistress, who left the school room leaving every body in apprehension of the events which would follow.

The first thing to do was to lock Reine up. Miss Gregor brought her to the punishment-room, a small room full of semi-darkness furnished with a wooden-table and a chair. Before leaving, she asked her:

— What happened?

— Miss Sticker was in my room, when I went back.

— So it's through me!

Reine would not lie:

— She took from my pocket a letter some one had written to me... to make caresses.

— One wrote to you?

— I can't help it.

— Why did you not tell me?

— I don't denounce.

— But you made me whip some of your companions.

— It isn't the same thing.

— What pupil was it?

— I won't answer, no more than as

though I was asked about you.

Miss Gregor understood that lust was dominating that girl.

— This affair will be the cause of a lot of harm to us.

— They can kill me, never shall I say what I won't.

Miss Gregor had to return to her pupils, and then went to Miss Sticker who vaguely remembered the text of the letter, and told her to bring her a writing-book of each child, to see if she could recognize the writing of the accomplice.

During Miss Gregor's absence, the pupils had concerted between themselves, not knowing wherefrom the danger could come. Miss Sticker certainly knew something, but what? None had a special appointment with Reine. Alexandra alone did not say anything and was very troubled when Miss Gregor took all the writing-books, they got calmer, for they knew they all had the same school hand-writing, as is usual in nearly all schools.

Besides, they now understood what the fault was. Alexandra remembered Reine had put her note in her dress pocket, and that letter must have been mislaid. She was anxious about the way she said she would put her legs. Eva remarked that it meant nothing, and that Miss Sticker did not suspect her. Besides, Reine knew better, and she had advised to deny, they only had all to deny, even called privately. It was in their interest. Pretend to be innocent would stop all accusations. They were then much quieter.

It was not the same with Miss Gregor. The school-mistress told her the nature of the note she had found, Reine's violence to take hold of it and destroy it, and her revolt against her authority.

Miss Gregor believed in her « gougnotte » as one believes in a true, deep and unique love. She remembered her adventure with Mary and why Reine had been sent away from France to get out of her mind the lust taught by a lady-cousin. But from a fanciful caprice their relationship had turned to a more powerful bond: she loved her and thought her voluptuousness would suffice. Everything was falling down now. She despaired of her slyness, when Reine swore their own felicities would content her for ever, and that she would not seek any anywhere else. Who was it? Perhaps a big girl? Miss Mary again?

What was the use of temper? Miss Gregor said she would often go to Reine to try and make her confess. It was a reason to speak with her, to show her her perfidy, to frighten her with the possibility of breaking with her. She was a woman after all, with charms not to be compared with the forms of a young girl, even amongst the big ones! She had illusions, as she could notice it at their first meeting.

Reine had begun work with courage. She did not feel any more pain on her behind. But while working she thought over Miss Sticker's spitefulness not understanding her conduct, after her weakness of the previous night, for she was sure the severe mistress had come up against her bottom. She was not frightened of the tortures in store for her, they were the rule of the house: the easel must be one of these tortures.

Unfortunately Miss Gregor approached her with these words:

— So then, Miss, when I thought I had all your attention, you were running after other petticoats!

— Miss Gregor, you are causing yourself some pain for nothing. Enquire what petticoats I could have been after. During the vacation, it was still possible. But now the surveyance is too great.

— Except in my school, where I showed you too much confidence.

— Confidence? Where you were sure of me by the pleasure that we had together! At school! Which one should I have addressed? All little girls. Do you compare yourself to these children?

The teacher could not help smiling.

— Who were you exchanging letters with? Miss Mary?

— Perhaps.

— Why not confess?

— You would have to repeat it to Miss Sticker.

— Is that the reason that keeps you back?

— Yes, darling Miss.

Miss Gregor made her sit on her knee:

— Do you still suffer?

— Hardly now.

She pressed her on her bosom, kissed her without a word, and went away. Such visits were several times repeated. She had an idea a big girl had tried to debauch Reine, and thought it stopped at the vicious amusement of an amorous correspondence.

At night, a servant took Reine back to her room. She went to bed, and thinking the survey would be doubled, did not even try to go to Miss Gregor's room. At half past nine, she was not asleep yet, when she saw Miss Sticker enter the room. Instinctively she brought her sheets right up her neck, to let her see she would not allow any « libertinage » with a woman who took so little notice of her « complaisances » of the previous night.

Miss Sticker sat by her bed and said:

— You did not sleep, Miss de Glady?

— I go to sleep late. Did you fancy to find me at fault again?

— No, you dare not. I called once again to know your accomplice's name.

— What does it matter to you, as you can punish me. And besides it is not right.

— What do you mean?

— Nothing. You understand I'm no fool, and if I have committed faults here, after I have committed them in France, I must have some experience about the vice of others, as hidden as they may be.

— You talk like a woman, and you interest me. So you have committed faults in my house? Tell me with whom. I'll send the culprit away, your accomplice, and will forgive you.

— With whom, murmured Reine smiling. Well, I'll tell you but you'll throw her away and I won't be chastised?

— I'll promise it.

— I committed a fault with somebody very strong, who jumped on my back, rubbed my cheeks with her bottom and who tried to tear a letter away from me. Do you know who it is, Miss?

Miss Sticker went pale under the mockery, but said:

— You are the demon's daughter, but the demon can be exorcised. I'll tame you. I've searched all day long. I don't want to keep in my house English girls débauché. You are French, I shall correct you in time. I have questioned Miss Gregor. She's sure your accomplice is not in your school, she thinks she must be amongst the big girls. It is not my opinion. I should rather think one of your companions... perhaps even your teacher. I shall find the rotten fruit, don't doubt it. So you had better confess, to evade the easel. Sooner or later I shall know your accomplice and nothing will prevent me sending her away.

— You know her, I told you just now.

— All right, Miss, to-morrow to the easel.

Miss Sticker went and Reine thought in herself: God help if she finds out Miss Gregor!

CHAPTER V

It is impossible to describe what Miss Gregor was suffering. Evoking the lust of the preceding nights and remembering Reine's audacious act in the school room her nerves vibrated, the blood was coming to her sexualities, and a terrible desire of lust was burning her, while she could not go to sleep. Her caresses were indispensable to her and she felt an afflux of heat to her vagina, cunt, clitoris, under a vision of her « gougnotte's » lips. She tossed herself off, and stopped under the bestiality of such act. Then she went to sleep, woke up early, and every one being asleep still, as she could not resist, she ran to Reine's room.

It was dark. Reine rested quietly. Miss

Gregor went to the bed and sat down. Now she was afraid, because 4 o'clock struck at the big clock. Supposing Miss Sticker would make a round! Never mind, she'd kill her. Reine awoke.

— Who's there?

— I, my beloved: don't be afraid. I had to come and see you. I want your caresses.

— You, Gregor! What a good idea you had. Lie down.

— Feel, if I'm warm!

She took one of the girl's hand and put it between her thighs, pushing one of her fingers to the clitoris.

— I believe I'll come with your touch only.

— No, no, come across my head, I will lick you.

In a second, Miss Gregor's thighs were as a collar round Reine's neck: the cunt was approaching her mouth, she took it, and all the teacher's sexuality was on her face. Reine sucked, sending her hands to catch hold of the cheeks, tickle the slit with her fingers... and the wet went over her.

— You did want it, my Gregor, you are wetting even my forehead. Don't move, I'll clean it and we'll start afresh.

The teacher was well on her back, the head near the heels, and Reine was pushing her tongue while one of her fingers was entering deep in the vagina, simulating the act of coït that she taught her thus.

Then Miss Gregor wished to lick and suck the girl who let her do it:

— Are you jealous, my Gregor?

— I'm dying of happiness and pain.

— I won't let you die! Oh! your tongue licks me well! I think I'll come to day.

— Whipping disposes to such pleasure, I told you. Oh, piss, piss your juice in my mouth.

— It's coming, it comes, oh! oh, isn't it nice, say, do you love my juice as I love yours?

— It's nectar itself. I'll compare presently, when you'll have made me come. You'll spare me some on your lips.

— Come quick, let me make it run from you. Let us profit. God knows what will happen to us. Miss Sticker passed in my room at the beginning of the night.

— She? here?

— Yes. She thinks I'm afraid of her!

Mistake. But be careful, she seems to suspect you.

— Me? Ah, don't let her try that or it'll end badly.

— Never mind about that. Place yourself well on me, so that I can suck all your flesh. Oh what Eden! to have my head between your thighs and under your bottom! I love it!

The lascivious caresses began again, but the coming was not so quick as at the beginning. They played with hands to toss off Reine. She had come, however, and did not want to any more, finding her voluptuousness in gestures and caresses, pursuing her dear teacher with the voracity of a bull-dog.

Her tongue went and went, and she was getting intoxicated with the sexual odour; she only left the clitoris to allow the lips to suck and all at once, using her nose, she pushed it right in the vagina, manoeuvring it as a man would have done with his prick. Was Miss Gregor ready? She squeezed her in her thighs so as to stifle her, and came, came, almost in convulsions, while Reine gathered up all the wet, and, getting away from the flesh-collar which kept her tight, jumped on her body, to wipe her own lips to hers, saying:

— Compare, Gregor.

— Love, oh, my love!

The tongues were getting mixed together, and woman and child were pressing one another in their arms. But time was flying, and Miss Gregor had to leave her « gougnotte ». Reine went to sleep again, caring nothing whatever for Miss Sticker and all punishments she could keep in reserve for her.

Next day, locked in the punishment room again, again she triumphed over the teacher's senses.

More Miss Gregor tasted her caresses, and more she desired them. Why refuse voluptuousness which was offered and which had become essential to her life? Never would she be able to go without them and live away from this girl who made of her a Messalina, thirsting for lust.

Miss Sticker did not show herself. She must have been very busy.

At her first visit to Reine, Miss Gregor, more enraged than if she had not been satisfied, came up, her skirts right up to the waist, with naked thighs and her audacious pussy underlining the whiteness of the belly.

— Quick, quick! you have time to make me come.

Reine left the table where she was at work and licked and sucked her heartily, caressing her cheeks with numerous « pattes d'araignée ». The desired sensation was not long to come, and Miss Gregor ran for her life, afraid at the thought that she might have been taken by surprise. Reine simply got up and resumed her work.

Every time the teacher came in again, the same game took place, and seemed natural to both.

At night, after meals, a servant told Miss Gregor that Miss Sticker wanted her to accompany Reine to the directorial office.

No doubt, it was for the punishment. Reine was greatly troubled, noticing the palor on Miss Gregor's face.

The school-mistress was waiting for them in a small parlour: she was calm, cold and austere in her looks.

— Will you, Miss de Glady, — for the last time — give me the name of the pupil who wrote to you?

— I have already told you, Miss Sticker.

— If I ask you a last time, it is to save you the shame you are going to be put to by exposure and correction before teachers and companions. Do confess. You are a thoroughly good pupil, and, decidedly, Miss Gregor must have been too lenient with you, as she has not noticed your fault: she'll have to suffer for it too in time. Don't be obstinate and confess.

— I can't say anything, although greatly touched by what you say.

— Remember your silence will not save your accomplice. I shall not assist in your torture, because, I don't want any silly back thought to remain in your mind. You understand me. My sister Gertrie will take my place.

— You won't preside, asked Miss Gregor?

— Do you question me?

— Oh, pardon!

— You refuse to speak out, Miss de Glady?

— I can't say anything.

— I'm sorry. Bring that child to the meditation room, Miss Gregor, where you'll put her in the hands of the servants to undress her. You'll call in, afterwards, all your pupils to the disciplinary room to make them assist to this culprit's execution on the easel. After the performance, you'll receive my personal instruction, now go!...

Miss Gregor took Reine's arm and took her away.

— What are they going to do to me, asked the child in great trouble.

— Bear everything with calm and resignation, this correction is more terrifying by the surrounding than by the pain. I have used you to flogging and beating, and you begin to feel the pleasure: don't cry, and if the pain overtakes you, think of me, because your cry would send me mad and I don't know what I should not do.

— No fear, Gregor, I would rather strangle myself than cry.

They arrived to the meditation-room, and two servants took Reine from the teacher's hands.

— Miss, said one, you must undress, all naked.

— All naked?

— You know it, you have already witnessed Miss Mary's correction and others.

Do it or we should have to do it for you by force.

— It's unnecessary. I'll undress. But it is a shame in a young girls' school, to show them naked to numerous eyes.

— Mademoiselle, said a severe, but sympathetic voice, you are the last to have a right to speak so.

— Mrs. Gertrie, said Reine.

It was Miss Sticker's sister who had entered the room. Beautiful brunet of twenty-eight, Gertrie Warlay was quite different from the school-mistress, in all her ways and looks. Several modifications in the school were due to her, although she was not often to be seen about the house, having more to do with the book-keeping department. Married to a naval officer who was away for long periods she had plenty of time to help her sister to look after her school and made herself very useful.

— Undress, said she, and cease all observation.

Humiliated, Reine obeyed. When naked, she was given sandals to put on and Miss Gertrie said:

— I am to preside your correction, Miss. I

hope that in accordance with your great fault, you'll submit to it without any clamour, and will not be an object of scandal to your companions. Nudity is not impudicity if one has no bad ideas. Please follow me. The servants will oblige you to it, if you refuse it.

— I don't refuse, Mrs. Gertrie.

Although very energetic, Reine became white when she entered the disciplinary room, when she noticed all eyes fixed on her. Through a mist she saw the teachers and their pupils, all seated before a sort of horse of very low height, made of wood or cardboard. Reine noticed Mary who seemed to be crying and Anna glaring at her in triumph. One made her stop before the horse, and Mrs. Gertrie said with irony:

— You'll be able to get on that noble animal, Miss, that will not kick in the least. However if you want any help one of the servants will do it with pleasure.

— I must get on that horse? What for?

— You are too curious. Will you get up?

— I am... ashamed, Mrs. Gertrie.

— So? Get her on it, Margaret.

A tall, stoutish servant caught Reine

under the arms and put her on the horse, close to its posterior. Reine noticed then that apparatus was made of india-rubber covered-up with velvet to soften the contact with the skin. As soon as she was in place two servants caught hold of her two legs, attached her with a solid leather belt to the back legs of the horse.

— Why am I tied up, asked Reine?

— You do ask questions! Wait now till I address a few words to the audience: Reine de Glady, having committed a fault of revolt against Miss Sticker who surprised her in fault with one of you, unknown up to now, is going to suffer flagellation by rod on this horse. If the accomplice chooses to denounce herself, Reine would have to suffer less, because the number of blows would be divided between the two culprits. If such accomplice is found afterwards, she'll be submitted to double the correction Reine is going to receive. Now be generous, who ever you are, Reine's accomplice. Say who you are!

No pupil spoke.

— Oh! it's too bad, said Mrs. Gertrie. Well, now finish attaching the culprit!

Reine was laid on the horse, her hands were tied with leather straps joined to the front legs of the apparatus, while another strap was tied to her waist, so that her cheeks were well « en relief » on the back part of the horse, while the thick part of the horse's tail was hiding her cunt.

She could not move, paralysed in all her members, with a vague perception that her bottom was high up as a mountain, above her body and that all looks were converging on it. And truly the bottom was coming out ever so much whiter because the sides of the horse were of ebony black and that her thighs were pressed, giving more rotundity to her shape.

When Reine was so exposed, each servant took a rod, and placed on each side of her they beat the cheeks of the girl's bottom in turn.

At the first blow, there was a movement of legs and arms; at the second one a shivering of the cheeks: the slit seemed to get right in, but Reine did not cry nor shout. The third and fourth blows brought on twistings of arms, tension of thighs, and the bottom tended to go right up.

The girl showed a terrible force of character. Poor little bottom! Teachers and pupils alike devoured it with their eyes, so much it was full of charm. But it did not call for pity!

Blows were going on rapidly, giving no time to the cheeks to feel the pain. They contracted, and the flesh was tinted with red, the arms were convulsing, and soon the whole body moved with tremendous efforts. Reine certainly tried to break her bounds. Blood was coming from every mark. Mrs. Gertrie got up and ordered to stop.

— You did not cry, Miss de Glady, we'll take it in account. You supported it all with courage. You will be carried to the infirmary, you'll be healed and in three or four days it will be all right.

When she was unbound, she fainted, she had given all her courage and was now done. She had to be carried away by the servants.

Mrs. Gertrie turned to the pupils and said:

— I'm sorry to say that there is someone amongst you who has not had heart enough, before such punishment, to confess she is the accomplice. But punishment touches sooner or later the culprit.

All the girls went out, moved by a same impression of pity and sorrow.

Alexandra had been often ready to cry out she was the accomplice, but her right and left hand side companions prevented her.

Sadness reigned now in all rooms and dormitories, for they all knew the French girl was unconscious in the infirmary and the interest came from the very point that very few knew what she was guilty of.

Miss Gregor had been kept back, and all girls gone, was to be punished also for her part of responsibility in the affair.

She was put all naked in a gallery and all teachers and servants could not help admiring her robust shape and forms. All of them, whip in hand, were guarding the different doors to stop any escape. Mrs. Gertrie, sitting in an armchair made a sign and one of the teachers came to Miss Gregor, slapped her bottom with the hand and said:

— Now, go and run.

Miss Gregor now ran all round the gallery passing before each other woman, who in turn whipped her hard on her naked flesh, on the bottom, the legs or the back.

The spectacle was very queer indeed.

She ran, getting her bust up, the waist accentuated over the open cheeks. The flesh was getting magnified in such a run and she developed herself in a voluptuous incarnation shivering under the whip of the « flagellantes ».

The blows were directed to the fleshy parts, and the clicking of the whip sounded hard. Now the teachers came nearer and nearer, taking pleasure to activate the action. She seemed to await such blows, to seek them, but her breath was giving way. At last she found herself encircled by the four teachers, she fell down on the floor; her shoulders, her back, cheeks, and thighs received the last blows and she did not move any more.

— Enough, said one of the teachers, dress yourself, Miss Gregor you may go back to your room.

It took her a while to get up, and then she had lost her balance, not by pain but under the impression of the pleasure of the finish that made her fall down. Every one helped her to dress, and she went away, knowing hardly how to walk.

And when once in her room, she thought of her little « gougnotte » at the infirmary...

CHAPTER VI

Reine had supported her torture with courage. From Mrs. Gertrie to any of the teachers, the opinion was on her side. If not hiding her vice, she did not revolt against the punishment.

At the infirmary, she was well looked after and soon came to her senses again. Suffering much less under the pain, she took her liberty of mind again. What more could they do to her?

She remembered the last blows, when a good warmth seemed to come to the very sources of her life, bringing almost ecstasy. Did she come, when she fainted or had pain knocked her down? She did not know. In the afternoon of the next day, she felt much better. The tearings were not serious and healed promptly. She could not see any one, and was only talking with the nurse. She wanted to go to her room again as soon as possible and to know if she should get any more punishment.

That evening, Miss Sticker came to visit her, and after inquiring after her health, asked her:

— Have you changed your mind, and will you speak out.

— I've had the correction. I have nothing to say.

— So you still have pity for a pig, who has let you suffer, even when there should have been a diminution of punishment, if she had denounced herself?

Reine did not answer. Had she not commanded the silence herself? Miss Sticker left her, without saying if corrections would be continued.

Reine wanted to leave the infirmary and see Miss Gregor as well as her companions again. Her blood stirred by the flagellation was all there again: she must have women and girls to quench her thirst of lust.

Never mind the punishment, she wanted

to make somebody come, and it was torturing her more than the desire to come herself.

Going to bed early, she turned and twisted in it: she could not sleep.

About eleven, one brought to the infirmary, a pupil feeling queer. It was not very serious, and some infusion of herbs did her a lot of good and she was left to rest.

Reine's mind was working. Was it one of her companions who had taken such pretext to join her? Her heart was beating. How could she know? She would have to wait until midnight, when the nurse would go to bed.

She was really born for lust. She called up all her reason not to commit a fault. Yes, the girl must have come there for her! But she did not move! Was she to face an indifferent girl, or really an invalid? Perhaps was it a trap? She must wait. But then she felt ticklings in her sexual parts she was ready for anything to satisfy her sensuality.

Half past twelve struck, she listened and heard the sound of sheets moved about. One was there for her, her kisses and licks and sucks, that she gave plenty. Bottoms, cunts, clitoris to toss off or to suck, she would never have enough of them.

The unknown person was also studying the situation. She saw her get out of bed and watch if there was no danger, inspect the room and so forth.

Who could it be? Never mind even the punishment of the horse, as long as she could lick the cheeks which were trembling with desire for her.

Would she open her curtains and run after her? Yes, but if she made a mistake? She waited. No, it was no mistake. A body was going about through the room, looking between the curtains of each bed.

She was wanted!

All at once she saw a shade, she turned round, ready to jump at the feet of the visitor, but she hardly stopped a cry of stupefaction? Her dread enemy, Miss Anna Bodirog, was in her nightgown standing before her.

Reine, deceived, simply said:

— Go away.

— No, I have something to propose.

— I do not forget the vacation.

— Don't be silly. Listen. I can be useful to

you.

— You wish to offer me money like you did Mary.

— Let me speak. I care not a fig either for Miss Sticker or her teachers. Besides I'm leaving in a week, to be married to a Frenchman, a country fellow of yours. I come to propose you to denounce me as your accomplice. I cannot be punished now I'm leaving and your punishment will be finished. Otherwise you'll be locked up alone, until she is discovered, and besides on any slight mischief you'll be corrected most severely.

— You would denounce yourself?

— I offer it.

— And why?

— Mary told me how you knew to make one come, make me come.

— You?

— I think I am giving you a good mark of friendship to have your caresses so sweet. Oh, I'll give them to you too, if you like.

Reine was thunderstruck! Indeed her desire was still burning! But to procure pleasure, coming, with the very girl she hated so much! Anna thinking that the best ways are the extreme ones, pulled up her chemise up to her neck, showed her pussy black and well furnished, brought Reine's hand to it, and the French girl let her do it.

— Now then, Reine, this is burning for you. Isn't it hot? We have detested each other wrongly, for I fancy I was the only girl capable of understanding you! Perhaps am I not so handsome as Mary, but my senses are more ardent and I possess more will in the piggish ways. Approach, don't resist, you want it, your little finger is feeling, yes there, it is on it.

Reine had felt conscientiously, and the finger tickled already the clitoris:

— All right, we'll play together, but what proves me that you will denounce yourself?

— If you doubt, we have only to be surprised in the same bed.

— They'll beat me again!

— No, they would correct me! Ah, tickle there, softly!

— Don't let us begin thus! All right I'll make you come, but take your chemise off and come into my bed. I'll leave mine. You understand we must get well prepared.

— You are right, and we'll adore one

another after.

Anna's chemise was soon at her feet. She got into the bed without a noise, and at once the two young bodies embraced each other, by legs and arms.

Their clitoris were also seeking each other, and a first kiss was exchanged. Reine murmured:

— Toss me off as I am doing you, and give me your tongue as I am giving you mine.

The French girl was expert: Anna shivered under the touch of the hand only between her thighs.

Reine had placed her whole hand on the cunt, and from there sent a finger to tickle the bud: her tongue was pointing between Anna's lips going far in.

Anna imitated all the manoeuvres of Reine.

— You are wetting, said Reine, now I have faith in you. I'll make you come. Open well your thighs so that I can put my head in the right place.

Anna had played with Mary, but both came little in their lesbian relations: therefore she did not expect such rapid pleasure.

When she felt Reine's face and mouth all over her cunt, she shivered and came with a convulsion of the whole body. She fainted almost when the girl's tongue wiped all her dew. And it was only beginning. Reine did not leave the place; she sucked the clitoris and with her hands under the bottom, tried to push a finger in the anus. Anna was getting high up, turned round and presented her bottom, thinking Reine wanted to lick it. A clever tongue went all over the slit, and then some « pattes d'araignée » put a vertigo in Anna's senses. All of a sudden she felt Reine's finger pushed right in her bottom-hole: another convulsion and she came a second time, whispering:

— Oh you are more than what I thought! You kill me, come into my arms.

Reine got higher up quickly, and Anna pressed her on her bosom.

— I ought to love you, instead of Mary.

The French girl was happy: her antipathy changed involuntarily and she felt a double pleasure to feel vibrating under her caresses, that English girl who had despised and hated her.

— How could I guess it. If you had asked

me, I should have not refused. I like it.

— Darling, when I'll be married, in France, we'll meet again.

— Alas, I am not returning there, yet a while.

Anna was still feeling her:

— You are more advanced than I in shape.

— I'm precocious: the cousin who taught me to suck used to say so. But you have gained since last summer: your cheeks are full and your hair has grown much.

— True, you like to caress me! Never has Mary's tongue produced an effect on me like yours.

— Because she does not understand the pleasure to tickle the bud, to let the saliva run in the bottom slit, and excite the one you hold under hands and lips. Shall I begin again frontward or backward?

— No, let me give you your licks back. Your bottom is so nice, I want to love it.

— Let us get on one another in an inverted way, and lick one another at the same time.

They placed themselves in sixty-nine fashion, Reine above: both Anna's hands caught hold of the cheeks and opened the slit. Reine let her do it and kept her own tongue on the clitoris: their caresses were the same and mutual. They licked, tossed off, and defied one another who would do it the longest.

If Reine wanted anything at the beginning of the night, she received more satisfaction than though she had had something to do with any other of her companions: Anna was coming over and over again, acting on her little friend who felt the voluptuousness announcing the coming of the spunk. Reine came indeed, as she only did with Miss Gregor. And such coming terminated the duet of lust. They had decided not to separate, and went to sleep embraced. They feared nothing: Reine had expiated and Anna was leaving the following week to be presented to her fiancé.

The nurse caught them thus in the morning. She stood dumbfounded at such sight, and, as the girls did not wake up, she retired without a noise and went at once to Miss Sticker.

Did the school-mistress understand what had happened, was she tired of such silly adventure? Anyhow she thought to reduce it as much as possible, and said:

— Two children who wanted to sleep together. Or have we here before us the accomplice who has invented such a way to denounce herself! Or is it a case of morbid hysteria, that the interest of my school commands me to hush up? I forbid you speak to anybody of what you saw. This house has always been honestly known, and will remain so. It is not an isolated case of momentaneous mania that would tarnish such reputation. Come, I'll follow you.

Miss Sticker took a whip with her and both went to the infirmary, where they found the two lovers still asleep. The shape of a bottom could be seen under the sheet, and down came the whip on it. It was Anna, who had been hit: she jumped out of bed with a cry, and ran away, pursued by Miss Sticker who was still whipping her hard on the cheeks of her bottom and thighs.

— You damned débauché, go back to your bed at once, and we'll have an explanation!

Reine was under the sheets, and the nurse was walking in Miss Sticker's footsteps.

— Where's your chemise?

— Over there, answered Anna, and I forbid you to hit me, you understand.

Miss Sticker's eyes were brilliant with rage, however she said calmly to the nurse:

— Bring the chemise of Miss Anna, and watch that nobody comes in here.

Reine could hardly believe in her luck: they had forgotten her. She had time to invent some story and while the nurse brought back Anna's chemise, she quickly put her own on.

Anna looked impertinently in Miss Sticker's face, and said:

— You wished Reine's accomplice to denounce herself. Could I decently do it before all your pupils, sowing ideas in their minds? I thought, thus acting with prudence, doing the best, and wishing also adieu to my dear little Reine.

— It was you, then!

— Yes. Reine pleased me, and since the vacation, I was running after her. She wouldn't, I forced her.

— It's a lie! It was Reine running after you. She has been punished. Now, for you...

— I'm leaving your school, to be married.

I am no more under your rules.

— You're mistaken, Miss Anna, you are under my authority, as long as you are with me.

— All right, give me the horse, and I'll shout that it is because I have débauché Reine, and you'll judge of the effect... in the future.

— I have no intention of fixing such or such punishment. But I can't leave you amongst your companions. I shall advise your parents to take you away without delay, and until your departure, you'll live under my sister's supervision.

— As you please. But for Reine, forgive her!

— That's my business. Dress yourself and I'll bring you to Mrs. Gertrie.

Miss Sticker then came back to Reine:

— You have received the correction you deserved. I am inclined to think this morning's surprise has been a « coup de theatre » managed by your accomplice. I will shut my eyes and forget. Go back to school and my desire is that nobody should know anything about what happened here. I'll speak to Miss Gregor.

— Oh, no, don't say anything to her.

— Why?

— Because... I should be corrected again.

— I'll forbid her to do so.

The two girls dressed, and when Anna was ready, she went to the door, saying loudly:

— Good-bye, Reine, don't forget me. I shall never forget you.

Miss Sticker's blood went to her face, and the whip was raised. Was she going to hit Reine or Anna? She did not move. Reine did not answer and was doing her hair, as usual, without any objection on the part of the school-mistress. The French girl was resuming her courage, seeing that there was no more chance of danger. And it was with a smile she said to Miss Sticker that she was ready.

— I'll accompany you to your school-room, said the school-mistress.

The whip was left in the infirmary and both went to the school-room. The scholars looked up very curiously. Reine resumed her seat unmoved, but winked at Miss Gregor to whom Miss Sticker was talking. She noticed the teacher looking at her with astonished and then severe eyes. After Miss Sticker's departure, the glance was as terrible as ever on Miss Gregor's part.

Reine looked around her: May was still her neighbour, but Alexandra had been changed to another place, near Eva. She tried to catch Alexandra's eye, but the girl pretended not to notice it. Reine finished up by ignoring such conduct and thought of Miss Gregor only. Certainly the teacher was wild at her love duet with Anna, as she was to have proof of it, a little later on.

As Reine was one of the last at the door, she trod unfortunately on Miss Gregor's foot, which was put there purposely, and the teacher slapped her face, and exclaimed in a temper:

— Be careful where you walk, Miss. You trod on my foot.

Reine was astonished, and she cried with rage. She was going to jump on Miss Gregor but her companions prevented her.

— I forbid you to slap me, you hear! You can martyrise my bottom, but no one must touch my face. I won't go to school, and wish to complain at once to Miss Sticker. We'll see what will happen!

Suffocating, Miss Gregor answered:

— Don't make any noise, Miss Reine, it was a movement of impatience, because you have hurt me. I apologize. Go to the schoolroom.

— Come on, Reine, said May, giving her a meaning look.

Reine did not insist, and obeyed: she was rewarded for it. The head school-mistress of the division, Mrs. Clary was especially amiable with her. Her fault was forgotten, and every one was trying to treat her gently. During the recreation, she was allowed to amuse herself with her companions, shake hands with Alexandra, who thanked her heartily for having spared her a correction for not denouncing her. Miss Gregor's looks were repentant, and Reine now tried to make her jealous, by going to chat with the other teachers.

She was full of joy, going back to the class room, for she noticed every one being good to her. Her punishment had evoked desire all around her. She had a proof of it, when she went to the riding-lesson. As she was passing by the teachers' lavatory, she came across Mrs. Clary who was coming out of it, and who, on the door, looked right and left, asking her:

— You go very quick, Reine, why?

— I'm going to the riding-room.

— Ah! really, and you don't want to...

— No, not at all, said she smiling.

— Are you sure?

— Oh, yes. Besides, it is not the place of the pupils.

— I would have authorised you to go to it.

— Only to see, then?

She went in, followed by Mrs. Clary very pale and excited.

— Now then, make your little pepe, and run away.

— That's not why you told me to come in.

— Yes, yes.

— I don't want to. Let us go, somebody might come.

— Will you watch me making my pepe?

— You don't want to, but show me what you do it with!

— Oh, little demon, you are not corrected?

Reine grew impatient at such talk.

— All right, I'll try to make pepe, and

you'll watch me, said Reine, as you don't want me to.

— Yes, yes, look, darling, it is through here.

— I know.

Mrs. Clary had pulled up her skirts and showed legs without drawers, a well-furnished pussy, and thick lips at the cout. Reine put her hand on it:

— Don't move, I'll give you a few licks, and we'll go.

Mrs. Clary shut her eyes, trembling with desire and fear. The girl's tongue was tickling her, she sighed and whispered:

— Enough, run away, little devil.

Her skirt fell down; Reine understood it was enough for once, and ran away. Even the head mistress succumbed to the temptation.

When back at school, Miss Gregor sat by her, and said softly:

— It is not right what you did at the infirmary: I suffered for you and you deceived my affection.

— No. Speak not so loud. Miss May might hear.

— I don't care. I have decided to leave

this house, where I am committing a crime in encouraging your vice, and losing my health.

— Shut up, don't say that. Go back to your desk, Miss Gregor, May is listening.

— The whip if she does not look at her work.

May was looking up indeed, wondering if she would not once more forget herself before the school.

Miss Gregor understood she was going too far. She followed Reine's advice and went to her seat again.

Soon after, the teacher was called by Mrs. Gertrie, and the pupils were left alone. Reine saw with surprise Alexandra disappear under Eva's skirts.

— Hullo! said she, my ex-neighbour likes it!

Eva, who had pulled up her skirts answered:

— She does it nicely with her tongue, but not so nicely as you, still it tickles.

May had got up, and skirts up, showed her bottom. Getting the cheeks out of the drawers, she said to Reine:

— My little bottom is thirsty of your

caresses. Give them quick.

Promptly Reine was on her knees, pushing her tongue in the slit, caressing the rotundities, and tossing her off with the hand.

May was twisting under the action, and moved her bottom about, such a bottom so appetizing and full of savour.

Eva sent Alexandra back, saying:

— I want to compare with Reine's caresses. Say, May, give me your place.

— You won't have time.

— Take Alexandra who is a good pupil of Reine, and we'll both enjoy it.

— What about us? cried a few voices.

— Do it between you, if you like.

— No, no, there's only Reine for that.

Reine had already her head between Eva's thighs, licking the cunt wet with Alexandra's kisses, as Alexandra was licking May's bottom wet with Reine's saliva. Eva was coming, and shouted:

— Ah, she uses more power. Oh! beloved little pig! I am pissing with pleasure, and she swallows my pepe. Oh! I'm dying, it is better even than before.

A shiver went over all the girls. Lisbeth

gave the alarm, and work was resumed at once. Miss Sticker came in and noticed Eva standing up at her desk. She said nothing, sat at Miss Gregor's desk and compared notes. The pupils were afraid.

The teacher came back, spoke a few words to Miss Sticker who went away. When gone, the teacher called Miss Eva to her desk:

— What is it, miss?

— Come here, and pull up your skirts.

— But...

— Obey, and show me your cheeks, you'll have the whip.

— What for?

— Shall I send you to ask it from Miss Sticker?

Eva obeyed, got her posterior out and presented it to Miss Gregor, who had the whip in hand.

— Don't hit hard, miss, please.

— Are you directing the correction? You know you were surprised in fault. Why were you standing up at your desk?

— To make with Alexandra what you do with Reine.

The whip fell from Miss Gregor's hands.

— With Alexandra!

— Whip me, but not too hard, and do not be afraid.

— Are you the mistress or I?

— You certainly, Miss Gregor. But you can divide the whipping between Alexandra and me, and even Reine, for the other day...

— Shut up.

Eva was still holding up her skirts, but received only little slaps with the hand, which seemed to be more so as to feel the flesh, and the girl approached herself complacently.

— Alexandra, come here, ordered Miss Gregor.

— Oh, Eva, you are spiteful.

— Will you come at once.

— Yes, Miss.

— You deserve to be corrected as well as Eva: pull up your skirts, and show your bottom.

— Yes, Miss.

Alexandra obeyed: her cheeks as white and plump as those of Eva showed out of the drawers and Miss Gregor said:

— The dark one and the fair one are balancing. Place yourself here, Eva, and you there, Alexandra.

Both bottoms were facing each other.

— Ah, you take the liberty of touching one another, there take that.

Two blows not hard came down on the bottoms.

— Which one was debauching the other?

— I told you, Miss, said Eva. Alexandra does to me what Reine does to you.

— You have a sharp tongue, your whipping will be double.

Two blows fell on Eva, stronger this time and reddening the flesh.

— Ah, Miss Gregor, you would act more justly in going back to your desk and calling Reine over like the other day.

— What a gossip; now your accomplice's turn.

The whip fell on Alexandra's cheeks, not hard, and she rounded her back, putting the two cheeks fully out of the drawers.

— Oh, the little devil, said Miss Gregor, one would think she is begging for the correction!

The whip went up again, the blows caressed gradually, more than chastising the bottom of the débauché. Suddenly the teacher put her hands between the thighs of the girl and said:

— Little pig, is that the effect of the punishment? I should have never thought you had such a nature!

Alexandra had put her hands to her eyes to hide her blushing: she had come under the whip.

Silently Miss Gregor caught her clitoris, tickled it and Alexandra came for the second time.

— Very well, said the teacher, taking her hand away. You also are at fault, Reine, so it seems. Come here. Give me your bottom, and I'll chastise it.

— But, Miss Gregor.

— You answer?

— Oh, no!

Reine came over and took place near Eva and Alexandra. This time they were all three in a row, and the teacher passing behind manoeuvred the whip on the three bottoms, making the girls bend to develop the rotundities. The three posteriors were consenting to it with docility and Miss Gregor was enjoying such view. The blows now transformed in ticklings, bringing shivers on the charming backs. It was no torture, that flagellation, but a great pleasure.

— Really, Eva and Alexandra, you pretend to imitate the games of your teacher with Reine? What does it all mean? Do you like the whipping then? And you Reine, what is the matter? Oh! are you losing your mind? You will take your revenge. Oh, she is as strong as a turk! Reine, obey! You won't, all right, there's the whip, here is my bottom, whip me, I authorise you.

— Hush, Miss Gregor, cried Lisbeth. Someone is coming. Miss Gregor who had pulled up her dress, showing her ample bottom, let the skirts fall down again and was hitting hard the three girls' bottoms.

Mrs. Clary entered, exclaiming:

— What is the matter here?

— I am correcting three girls at fault. That's enough, go back to your desks.

The girls were glad to obey.

Mrs. Clary went to Miss Gregor and whispered:

— What again, that poor Reine? There is decidedly an animosity against her.

— Not at all! She deserved a new

correction and she submitted to it without a murmur. What is it you want, Mrs. Clary?

— I just came about her! Three evenings a week after meals, shall I give her a private lesson, to gain the lost schooling.

— You will give her private lessons, I could have done it myself.

— It is Miss Sticker's orders.

— All right, I'll send her to you.

— You heard, Reine? said Mrs. Clary, I hope you'll work in consequence.

— Yes, Madame, you can rely on me.

Mrs. Clary went away and Miss Gregor began to think what would happen now her passion was known to all the pupils. Lisbeth's intervention also proved her a sort of entente between all the girls, looking so innocent and chaste.

Her eyes were going all round the room. Reine was biting her pen-holder and looked up at her. Oh, the perversity of her cheeky hair! And these lascivious eyes! She seemed to mock her, why should she not also mock her too? Wasn't it long since the lips of her « gougnotte » had been on her cunt and clitoris! And now that Mrs. Clary was delaying the joy she dreamt of for that very evening!

Would she perhaps feel that joy? Would the girl not be too tired after the lesson? No, she could not wait any longer, she must come over the head of that French girl, who guessed her thoughts.

What was she doing? Leaving her seat now, without her permission, coming to her own desk! She feared nothing! What cheek! She was standing up before all the pupils, saying to Lisbeth:

— Be on the watch!

Oh, joy of all joys! Reine knelt down between her thighs, mesmerising her with the game of her tongue. She pulled up the teacher's skirts and kissed the vagina. A mist went over her eyes, she was wetting, coming, she, the very guide of these girls! She murmured:

— Alexandra do it to Eva!

Reine stopped licking and sucking, got up between her thighs, and the head above the desk ordered:

— Eva, come here and look!

Miss Gregor was herself no more. She wanted to revolt, was coming under Reine's hand put on her clitoris and cunt, Reine's hands pushing her belly back, so that she could remain prostrated in her armchair, the thighs right in front.

Eva obeyed to Reine, and came near the desk. Then, the « gougnotte » opening the teacher's legs, and pulling the skirts far above the waist, said:

— Look, how nice she is and see how she comes! All that is mine. I willingly leave you Alexandra, but let her do it near here.

— Reine, Reine! murmured Miss Gregor, I'm lost.

— Don't be afraid, Lisbeth is on the watch.

— Ah! ah! let them all do it if they like.

— No, Eva and Alexandra only, said Reine. I am the mistress.

— So you are, whispered Miss Gregor, throwing her legs round her neck. Toss me off, suck me and kill me.

END OF THE SECOND VOLUME

BIRCHGROVE PRESS
Flagellant & Libertine Erotica

———

Birchgrove Press specializes in producing new print and e-book editions of pre-1950s writings on sexual flagellation in English. Original editions of many of the books that we offer are difficult to obtain and are highly sought after. We are especially proud to offer new editions of rare Victorian flagellant texts such as *The Mysteries of Verbena House*, *Experimental Lecture by Colonel Spanker*, and *The Quintessence of Birch Discipline*. Birchgrove Press also produces new editions of libertine literature. We have published *Venus in the Cloister, The School of Venus, The Dialogues of Luisa Sigea*, and Isidore Liseux's translation of the Marquis de Sade's *Justine* (1791), *Opus Sadicum*, for example.

www.birchgrovepress.com.

www.ingramcontent.com/pod-product-compliance
Lightning Source LLC
Chambersburg PA
CBHW072004170626
46813CB00005B/2005